The Adventures of Lily L

By

Barbara Park

Illustrated by John Wotherspoon

Includes Activity Suggestions

AuthorHouse™
1663 Liberty Drive
Bloomington, IN 47403
www.authorhouse.com
Phone: 1-800-839-8640

First published by AuthorHouse 07/18/2011

ISBN: 978-1-4567-8648-9 (sc)

Printed in the United States of America

Any people depicted in stock imagery provided by Thinkstock are models,
and such images are being used for illustrative purposes only.
Certain stock imagery © Thinkstock.

This book is printed on acid-free paper.

authorHOUSE®

Lily was a leaf. She was very proud to be a leaf on the big tree in the park and all summer long she waved gently in the breeze watching the children playing in the grass below and across on the other side of the park in the school playground

She loved the feel of the sun on her face

And thought the little rain drops which pitterpattered onto her, through the leaves further up the tree, tickled.

One day she suddenly realised that the sun wasn't quite as hot as it had been and then she noticed a sort of brownish spot on her coat.

"How did that dirty mark get there?" she thought and the next time it rained she rubbed it hard to try to clean it away.

"What are you doing?" the leaf next to her asked. "I'm trying to get this mark of my coat" Lily replied. "That won't wash off", said the leaf, "it's the start of autumn".

"What's autumn?" asked Lily. "Don't you know?" said the leaf in a very surprised voice. "No" said Lily quietly. She was beginning to be a bit worried; she didn't like the sound of autumn.

"Well" said the leaf, "in autumn our coats start to change colour. Most of us end up a horrible brown colour and then the wind comes and this isn't like the gently summer breeze we've all enjoyed waving in, oh no, this is a really fierce wind which makes our tree sway and the wind will rip us from our twigs and we will be blown away. Eventually we will end up lying down t h e r e on the g r a s s a n d the Park Keeper will come and sweep us up onto a bonfire".

By the time the leaf had finished talking, Lily was crying and very, very frightened. "I don't believe you," she whispered.

"It's true" the leaf said, "Mr Robin told me, he saw it all last autumn". Lily didn't want to believe the leaf, but Mr Robin was very wise.

Every day she watched her coat, sure enough more spots started to appear, but they weren't all brown, some were a lovely shade of red and others were more of an orangey colour.

When she looked around at the other leaves they were all changing too, but secretly she thought that she looked far prettier than they did. She didn't say anything though as she was a kind leaf and didn't want to hurt them.

Gradually the wind started to get stronger.

Lily felt herself being tossed about on her twig. She
noticed some of the other leaves being pulled away and
was very frightened.

She held on as tightly as she could, until she couldn't hold on any longer and with a little cry she felt herself being pulled away from the tree and suddenly she was flying through the air.

She went sailing across the park. If she hadn't been so frightened she thought that she could have found it quite good fun.

Then suddenly, BUMP, she hit a wall and landed on the ground. "Ouch! That hurt," cried Lily. She looked about and realised she was lying not far from a big lump of grass and there were other leaves there as well.

She was just starting to feel a bit better when she heard voices. They seemed to be coming from the lump of grass and as she watched 2 beetles appeared dragging leaves behind them.

"These leaves will make a lovely lunch" she heard one of the beetles say. Lily started to shake again. "I don't want to be eaten," she thought -

-but then a big gust of wind came and she found herself flying through the air again.

"Oh thank you Mr Wind," she cried. This time she flew over a road towards some houses and -

-landed, splat in a pond. "Ooooh! I don't like this, its wet and cold," she said.

"Well you are in my pond," said a voice, and there below her was a big goldfish.

"Hello" said Lily "I'm sorry to disturb you. The wind blew me here and I would like very much to get out. Please will you help me?"

"I'll see what I can do," said the goldfish and he started to push her gently across the pond with his nose. It tickled a bit, but Lily didn't mind.

Slowly the goldfish pushed her to some stones at the edge of the pond and then with one final big push she found herself lying on top of one of them.

"Thank you, Oh thank you so much," she cried. "Your welcome", said the fish. "Just lie there for a few minutes in the sun and dry off. Good luck." And off he swam.

Lily did as she was told. She could feel the sun on her and gradually she began to feel warm and dry again.

"I wonder what is going to happen to me now" she thought. She hadn't forgotten about the Park Keeper's bonfire and didn't want to end up there.

Suddenly she was up in the air again, sailing across the houses and roads, but this time she fluttered to the ground and didn't hurt herself at all.

She seemed to be in a garden.

It was very pretty, with lots of plants. She could see a
little girl wandering around.

The girl seemed to be looking for something. Slowly she came nearer to Lily and then suddenly she gave a cry of delight and swooped down and picked Lily up.

"Mummy, Mummy, I've found one. It's beautiful and just what I need for my picture".

Lily didn't understand what was happening to her. She felt herself being carried into the house and then the little girl was showing her to a grown up and saying "Isn't it lovely".

"Does she mean me?" thought Lily. Then she heard the grown-up say, "Yes Mary, it is a beautiful leaf and will make your picture very special. Let's stick it on now".

Lily was turned over and something sticky was put on her back. Next she felt herself being pushed against something and when she looked around she seemed to be stuck to some paper along with some twigs and a few leaves.

Then she was pushed into a dark thing and felt herself being carried along. "What is happening to me now," thought Lily, but eventually the dark thing was opened and Mary pulled her and the paper out.

Lily realised she was in a classroom of the school she had been able to see from her tree.

Everyone was looking at her and agreeing with Mary that she was really beautiful.

The teacher took the paper and pinned it up on the wall.
Finally Lily realised she was safe.

She could forget about the horrible bonfire. She was going
to stay in the classroom with all the children who kept
smiling at her and she smiled back and gave a big happy
sigh.   THE END

SUGGESTED ACTIVITIES

1. The following leaves are shown on Page 25, do you know which is which? Beech, Birch, Elder, Hawthorn, Holly, Horse Chestnut, Oak, Pine, Sycamore.

2. Which two of these leaves don't change colour, like Lily did, in Autumn? Do you know why?

3. Why don't you go and find some leaves and make a collage, like Mary did, in the story!

4. Can you draw a picture of Lily and colour it in?

CPSIA information can be obtained
at www.ICGtesting.com
Printed in the USA
2588LVUK00002B

9 781456 786489